DATE DUE

OCT 05 2010		
NOV 10 2011		
OCT 18 2012		
APR - 4 2013		
NOV - 8 2013		
SEP 12 2014		
JAN 29 2016		
SEP 16 2016		
JAN 31 2018		

Doorway to Darkness

by John Banks

ILLUSTRATED BY SONNY LIEW

Librarian Reviewer
Marci Peschke
Librarian, Dallas Independent School District
MA Education Reading Specialist, Stephen F. Austin State University
Learning Resources Endorsement, Texas Women's University

Reading Consultant
Elizabeth Stedem
Educator/Consultant, Colorado Springs, CO
MA in Elementary Education, University of Denver, CO

STONE ARCH BOOKS
Minneapolis   San Diego

First published in the United States in 2007
by Stone Arch Books,
151 Good Counsel Drive, P.O. Box 669,
Mankato, Minnesota 56002
www.capstonepub.com

First published by Evans Brothers Ltd,
2A Portman Mansions, Chiltern Street,
London W1U 6NR, United Kingdom

Library of Congress Cataloging-in-Publication Data
Banks, John, 1948 Mar. 1–
    [Gateway from Hell]
    Doorway to Darkness / by John Banks; illustrated by Sonny Liew.
    p. cm. — (Shade Books)
    First published: London: Evans Brothers Ltd., 2003 under the title
Gateway from Hell.
    Summary: While a group of people camps near a road
construction site in hopes of saving a hill that some believe holds a
terrible secret, a large predator begins roaming the area.
    ISBN-13: 978-1-59889-351-9 (library binding)
    ISBN-10: 1-59889-351-3 (library binding)
    ISBN-13: 978-1-59889-446-2 (paperback)
    ISBN-10: 1-59889-446-3 (paperback)
    [1. Supernatural—Fiction. 2. Protest movements—Fiction.
3. Environmental protection—Fiction.] I. Liew, Sonny, 1974– ill.
II. Title.
PZ7.B225935Doo 2007
[Fic—dc22   2006026873

Art Director: Heather Kindseth
Graphic Designer: Kay Fraser

Printed in the United States of America in Stevens Point, Wisconsin.
102009
005625R

TABLE OF CONTENTS

Chapter 1

PROTEST AT MOTT HILL

The yellow digger bit deeply into the side of the hill. With a roar of its engine, it backed out and turned. It tipped a load of dirt and stones into a waiting dump truck.

A high fence with barbed wire at the top was a safe distance from the work. A crowd of people shouted and waved banners on the other side.

"Stop the road now! Don't kill our countryside!" they yelled.

A row of police officers and security guards in yellow coats stood on the working side of the fence.

More guards were waiting behind the protesters in case of trouble. They had worked on the site of the new road for months now. They knew that today would be the biggest protest yet. The machines were digging a path through Mott Hill.

Mott Hill was a special place.

The shouting of the crowd grew louder and angrier as the digger cut deeply into the side of the hill. A bottle flew over the fence. A stone followed it. The police moved in.

Big Jim, one of the leaders of the protest, pushed into the middle of the crowd. "Keep it peaceful! Don't do anything stupid! You're just playing into their hands!" he yelled.

Things were getting out of control. The protesters were pushing on the fence, shaking it back and forth. Another stone flew over. It bounced off the helmet of a security guard. More police moved in. They started to make arrests.

Outside the fence, a reporter was busy finding people to interview.

An older man tried to make himself heard over the noise. He was big and muscular, with a bushy gray beard. "Mott Hill has always been special," he said. "Ancient people worshipped here. There was trouble before, when this ground was disturbed!"

"But only a very small part of the hill is being lost, and the road will fix local traffic problems," said the reporter.

"I don't have anything against roads," said the man. "But I tell you, digging here is dangerous."

Some of the loudest protesters were arrested, so the crowd began to calm down.

A tall girl with dark hair, who was named Lisa, looked around. She sighed with relief. Luke, her boyfriend, was still there. He had been arrested before. He always got angry about the way the countryside was being destroyed.

Lisa pushed her way through the crowd. Luke was right up against the fence, yelling at the busy workers.

"Vandals!" he yelled at them. "You're just vandals!"

Lisa tugged on his sleeve. He turned around. "Just making sure you're still here!" she said.

Just then there was a gasp from the angry crowd. Then people cheered. Luke turned back to the fence and stared.

The yellow digger had disappeared.

Chapter 2

THE DANGEROUS DIG

Evening came. The workers and most of the police officers went home. The protesters' camp was lit up with fires. It was early in the summer, and the nights were chilly. Lisa and Luke sat close to their fire, glad of the warmth. Lisa's dog, Raven, lay between them. Raven looked fierce, but he had never hurt anyone. He adored Lisa.

"It was amazing when the digger vanished down that hole," said Lisa. "I'm glad the driver wasn't hurt."

"It would have served him right if he had been, if you ask me," said Luke.

Lisa understood that the driver of the digger was just an ordinary man. He was just doing his job, even if they didn't agree with what he was doing.

Luke had always found it hard to control his anger. He had been through a lot in his life. He had never known his parents. He had spent his childhood running away from foster parents and children's homes. Luke wasn't easy to get along with. Lisa was his first real friend.

They thought back to the amazing events of the morning. When the big digger had moved farther into the trench, the ground had given way. Then the machine had slid into a huge hole in the hillside.

The driver had managed to climb out. A chain was fixed to the digger, and a giant truck pulled it out.

Work had stopped for the day. Nothing could be done until the hole was filled in.

Local scientists said that the hole had to be examined first, but that might take weeks. The road builders were not happy.

Big Jim was listening to a radio. He shouted for people nearby to be quiet.

"They're doing a news report on the protest. Listen!" he said.

They all listened to a report of the day's events. They knew that radio and TV were important. A group of protesters couldn't defeat the police and the road builders. They had to get their message across to the public.

The news show switched to an interview with the man who had spoken on the radio that morning.

"Harold Dyson is a local expert on Mott Hill. He has strong views on the new road," said a reporter's voice.

"As I have said many times, digging up Mott Hill is dangerous! Something is in there that must not be disturbed," said Mr. Dyson.

Luke groaned. "That guy's just a nutcase," he said.

Lisa got angry.

"Why can't you believe in something, Luke? There is something special about this hill. That's why we're here. Everyone can feel it, except you!" she said.

Luke didn't believe in anything but his own anger. He was about to give one of his hard and bitter replies, but he didn't get the chance.

A terrible scream cut through the dark night. It came from the direction of the road work.

Chapter 3

AFTER THE
ATTACK

Everyone in the protesters' camp began
to rush toward the fence to see what had
happened. Jim told some of the group to
stay at the camp, in case it was a trick by the
security guards. They might be planning to
wreck the camp while it was empty.

Down at the work site the floodlights
had been switched on. The protesters looked
through the fence. They could see one man
lying on the ground and other figures in
yellow jackets bending over him.

One of the men in yellow jumped up and came over to the protesters. He was so angry that he could hardly speak.

"Which one of you worthless scum did this? That's a good man there, hurt! Wait till I find out who did this!" he yelled.

Big Jim tried to calm him down.

"Look, man, we don't go around hurting people. Whatever happened to that guy, it wasn't us," Big Jim said.

The security guard wouldn't listen. He kept on yelling.

"He's a friend of mine. He's got a wife and young kids. All of you should be put in jail, or worse!" The man was shaking.

For once, the protesters were glad there was a fence.

Blue lights flashed on the road to the site. It was an ambulance and police cars.

"Let's get back to the camp," said Jim. "The cops have arrived, and there's going to be trouble."

The trouble came about fifteen minutes later, when the police stormed into the camp. A chief detective stood in the center. He spoke into a megaphone.

"A man has been attacked tonight," he said. "Everyone here is a suspect. No one will leave this camp until they have been interviewed by the police."

Another police officer walked into the camp. He spoke to the chief detective, who nodded and barked out orders. They started searching the tents and shacks, shining flashlights into every corner.

They ignored the complaints of the protesters who had started settling down for the night.

They flashed a light into Lisa's tent.

Raven growled.

"Over here, sir," said an officer.

The chief detective ordered Lisa to come out of her tent. Luke came out of his tent to see what was going on.

"Is this your dog?" asked the detective. "It looks like a dangerous animal to me."

"Raven wouldn't hurt anybody," said Lisa.

"Really? The injured man's throat was ripped by a large animal," said the detective. "Officer, get some help up here and take that dog away."

"Leave him alone!" cried Lisa. "I've told you, he wouldn't hurt anybody!"

But the police wouldn't listen to her. A special animal handler came and strapped a muzzle over Raven's mouth. Then the dog was dragged into a van.

Chapter 4

RAVEN

Lisa spent the night in tears. Luke tried to cheer her up. The trouble was, he wasn't very good at that sort of thing. He could handle police officers, but dealing with his friend was much more difficult.

Luke's tough life had made him hard. It wasn't easy for him to trust anyone, not even Lisa. No one had ever liked him much. People had always let him down. Maybe even Lisa would let him down in the end.

The next morning, Lisa was woken up by the sound of barking. Raven was back.

At first she thought he must have escaped, but a police officer was standing outside her tent with the dog on a leash.

"He's in the clear," said the police officer. "Forensics say the teeth marks on the injured man don't match your dog. They don't think it was a dog at all. And we've had more trouble. It happened when your dog was locked up, so it wasn't him."

He looked at Lisa. "You seem like a nice girl," he said. "How come you got mixed up with all these losers? Don't you have a home somewhere?"

Lisa was furious.

"They are not losers, and I don't have to listen to lectures from you!" she said.

The police officer held up his hands. "Okay, okay! Just take my advice."

Lisa smiled sweetly at him. "And whatever you say, I'll do the complete opposite," she said.

Lisa was happy to have Raven back, but everyone else in the camp was in a gloomy mood. Protests were one thing. A savage attack was quite another.

Later on, a truck pulled up in the camp. Two men got out. They looked angry. One of them was carrying a shotgun.

"Where's that dog?" said one of them. "I've got three cows with their throats ripped out. If the police won't deal with this problem, we will!"

Raven was lying in the sunshine, recovering from his scare of the night before.

One of the farmers spotted him. "There he is, Jack. Get him, quick!"

With a scream, Lisa jumped up and threw herself on top of the surprised Raven. The farmer tried to pull her off. Other people joined in, fighting with both of them.

The police had been expecting trouble. Six officers burst into the clearing, and the fight ended. Luke had been in the thick of the fighting. Two officers held him back.

"Come to help your friends?" said Luke, taunting one of the officers.

The officer turned and said, "When will you learn that we're here to protect you, just like everyone else!" He turned to the two farmers. "I'm placing you two under arrest," he said.

The farmers got angry.

"We've got a right to shoot dogs that kill livestock," said one of the farmers.

"Not here you don't," said the officer. "As for the rest of you, take my advice and leave. There's something bad going on. We don't know what it is, but it's a lot bigger than a dog and it's much more dangerous. I don't want anyone else getting hurt!"

Chapter 5

DYSON'S FEARS

After the police left, the protesters talked about what they should do next. Some people didn't believe the farmers. They thought it was just a trick to get rid of them. Others were frightened.

The camp and the road were full of reporters. One of them was Mike Short, who worked for the local radio station. The members of the group trusted him. He had always been fair. They asked him about the farmers' story.

"Yes, it's true," said Mike. "I've seen the cows myself. It was a real mess. One of them was completely ripped apart."

Lisa was thinking about the radio interview. She couldn't get it out of her mind.

"Mott Hill is dangerous!" the old man had said. "Something is in there that shouldn't be disturbed."

"That man you interviewed, where could I find him?" Lisa asked Mike.

"You mean Harold Dyson?" said Mike. "He's a strange guy! He lives over the hill by the post office."

Luke looked at Lisa.

"You mean the loser on the radio?" Luke sneered. "Don't make me laugh!"

Lisa got angry. Too furious for words, she went into the tent and gathered up her belongings. Luke tried to stop her.

"Lisa, I'm sorry," he said. "Really."

Lisa stormed out of the camp, taking Raven with her.

Harold Dyson was easy to find. He was sitting in his garden, looking through some old books. His big body and tangled beard made him look frightening. When he heard why Lisa had come, he welcomed her.

"This isn't the first time something like this has happened," he said. "I've been going through old history books. The last time was in 1868. People were digging for gold in Mott Hill, and a big hole was uncovered. Three people and many animals died then. The deaths stopped when the hole was filled in."

"But what killed the cows? And what attacked the worker?" asked Lisa.

"I don't know," said Harold. "The old books talk about monsters. Some people think that Mott Hill is not a natural hill. It was made by people. They say it was put there to stop these things escaping."

"Why don't you tell someone?" asked Lisa.

"I have told people. And what do they say? 'Harold Dyson is a crazy man.' They believe there's an animal escaped from the zoo that's doing all this." He snorted. "There isn't a zoo for miles around!"

"Then what can we do?" asked Lisa.

"Close up the doorway!" said Harold.

Lisa was confused. "What do you mean, the doorway?" she asked.

"That hole in the hill," Harold said.
"Lisa, I'm not a superstitious person, but
sometimes I wonder if it isn't a doorway
to the powers of evil!"

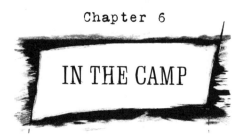

Chapter 6

IN THE CAMP

Later that afternoon, Harold and Lisa walked back to the camp. On the way it started to rain. By the time they got to the camp there was a steady drizzle.

The camp was full of noise and movement. The protest group had decided to move into the trees.

"We're not leaving," said Big Jim. "But if there is something dangerous prowling around, we'll be safer sleeping in the trees."

Lisa introduced Harold to the group. Luke was looking angry, so Lisa ignored him.

Luckily the tents hadn't been taken down yet. The protesters crowded into the largest one to hear what Harold had to say. They didn't all fit in the tent. Some people listened from outside, holding plastic sheets over their heads.

Harold told them what he had told Lisa. "What happened in 1868 is happening again. You can hide in the trees if you want. But there is no escape from them," he said.

There was silence for a moment. Then Ed, one of the tree platform builders, spoke.

"It's going to be a big job, filling that hole. You need machines for that," he said.

Then Luke spoke. "Not a problem. I can operate one of those diggers. I learned how during the last protest, and I don't need keys to start one up."

Some of Luke's friends laughed. They remembered where that digger had ended up. Luke was lucky he hadn't been caught.

"What about the security guards and the police?" someone asked.

"They're gone," said Luke.

Lisa went over to Luke. "I thought you didn't believe in all this," she said.

Luke smiled. "I don't," he said. "I just like driving diggers!" He laughed.

Harold was invited to stay in the camp until dark. That's when the raid would take place.

Jim would cut a hole through the wire fence. Then Jim, Luke, Lisa, and Harold would climb through. Luke would operate the digger. The others would light up the area with flashlights.

The rain fell all afternoon and evening. The group tried to keep dry. After dinner, the "task force" (as they called themselves) got ready to go. Lisa insisted that Raven come with them. She wouldn't let him out of her sight.

Luke heard a noise outside when he was putting on extra rain gear. "Quiet down, people. There's something outside!" he said.

They heard a strange sniffing noise, mixed in with hisses and grunts. Something was heading up the path from the wire fence.

"Into the trees!" Luke yelled.

There was a scramble to climb up into the trees. Raven had to be lifted up.

A creature was in the camp below. Lisa and Luke could hear it under their tree. It seemed to know they were there. It circled around, hissing and spitting. Raven was terrified. Lisa could feel the dog's heart beating fast as she held him.

With a great snarl, the beast jumped up at the tree. They heard huge claws scraping at the bark. The whole tree shook.

The creature couldn't reach them. It snarled once more, then went off to look for other victims.

"Quick," said Harold. "While it's gone, we can take care of the hole. Let's get moving!"

Chapter 7

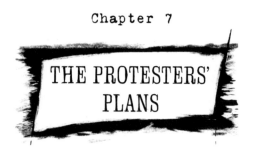

THE PROTESTERS' PLANS

The rain still poured down. Jim went first, with the wire cutters. There were no guards to stop him, so he soon made a large hole in the fence.

"Look at that!" said Big Jim.

Big Jim had noticed a hole right by the fence. Whatever the beast was, it had dug its way under. Harold examined it carefully by flashlight.

"It's huge," he said. "And look at those claw marks on the ground!"

The task force slipped into the work site. Diggers and trucks sat empty in the darkness. Luke went over to the nearest digger. The rest went and shined flashlights down the hole.

"Yuck, what a smell!" said Luke.

A terrible smell came up from the hole. There were more claw marks there, easy to see in the muddy ground.

Lisa had a sudden thought.

"Harold, we can't fill it in now. The creature is still outside. We need to wait until it comes back."

Harold shook his head. "No, fill it in! Trap the creature here."

"We'll deal with it later," Harold added.

Big Jim wasn't sure.

"What are we dealing with, anyway?" he asked. "I've got a bad feeling about the whole business."

Then they heard Luke calling. He came over with bad news.

"I can't start the digger," he said. "They put on some new security device."

"Okay," said Jim. "Pete, go and get everyone down here. There are shovels around, and pickaxes. We'll use our bare hands if we have to. We need to get this hole filled before that thing gets back."

"I'm on my way," said Pete, disappearing into the darkness.

The rest of the task force turned off their flashlights to save the batteries. It was frightening, standing there in the dark, knowing that the creature could return at any moment.

Luke thought he heard a sound coming from the hole.

They all listened carefully but heard nothing.

"Probably just a loose stone falling into the hole," said Harold. "But look. Can you see anything down there?"

They all looked. Their eyes were used to the dark by now. At the bottom of the hole they could see a faint light.

"Listen," said Luke. "There's that sound again!"

They all heard it this time. A hissing and scraping sound was coming from the hole, getting louder all the time.

Another creature was coming through the doorway.

Chapter 8

CREATURE FROM BELOW

The creature appeared before they had a chance to run. The protesters could see a shape in the dark. It walked on two legs, and was as tall as a human being. A terrible smell came from its body. Huge arms hung down by its side.

Everyone turned and tried to run toward the hole in the fence, but it wasn't easy running over the soft, sticky ground.

The creature snarled in anger. Its arm struck out at Luke, and he felt a hit on the side of his head. Luckily it had hit him with the back of its hand and not with its claws.

Suddenly Pete arrived with everyone from the camp. They all shined their flashlights on the creature from the other side of the fence.

The beast was dark brown and scaly, with a face like a wolf. Its eyes were huge. White slime hung from its jaws. A tail dragged along the ground. If there were such creatures as aliens, this must have been one of them.

The creature seemed to hate the light. It covered its blinded eyes with its arms.

Lisa could feel herself slipping in the mud. The creature was right behind her.

She felt a terrible pain. The claw scratched her shoulder through her coat as she sprawled on the ground.

At that moment, Raven jumped. He had seen the beast attack his owner, Lisa. The dog sank his teeth into the beast's scaly leg.

The blinded creature couldn't see what was hurting it. It let out a dreadful howl. From behind the people by the fence came another howl. The other creature had come back.

There was instant panic. Everyone was desperate to escape. Running this way and that, they stumbled off through the woods, taking their flashlights with them.

Now the creature could see again.

Frightened by the savage bite from Raven, it rushed toward the tunnel under the fence. Raven chased it, barking loudly.

Lisa managed to get up again. "Raven! Come back!" she yelled.

The creature coming down the path was much braver than the one that had hurt Lisa. It forced its way through the hole in the fence.

Harold was still standing near the hole. The new creature decided to make him a target. Harold cried out in alarm. He could barely see the creature's shape in the dark, but he knew that the sharp claws were coming toward his face.

Suddenly there was the roar of an engine.

The generator! The floodlights flickered and came on. The whole scene was as bright as day. The creature screamed and put its paws over its eyes. With a huge leap, it reached the hole and slipped down inside.

Harold was blinded too. He took a step back and slipped on the wet mud. He started to slide feet first down the hole. There was nothing to hold on to, to stop him from falling.

Lisa was the nearest person. She threw herself down on the ground and grabbed his hands, just as they disappeared over the edge of the hole.

Harold was too heavy for her, but she wouldn't let go until she felt herself sliding down as well.

When she did let go, it was too late. She was sliding head first down the hole, with no idea how deep it was or what was at the bottom.

Chapter 9

WHERE'S LISA?

The foreman, the head of the workers, did not believe a word of the strange story. He had heard all the noise from his office down the hill and had turned on the lights. When he got up the hill, the action was all over.

"Monsters? Do you expect me to believe that? I believe what I see with my own eyes. And I see serious damage to a fence," he said.

He looked at the digger.

He added, "Someone tried to mess with this machine, too."

He talked into a small radio. "Ted? Bring the guys up here, okay? More trouble. And call the police."

For the first time in years, Luke's hard shell broke down. He was in tears.

"Look, I'm telling you, my girlfriend fell into that hole," he said. "She might be hurt. She needs help."

The foreman sighed.

"This had better be true," he said. "I know you people. You'll do anything to cause trouble."

Big Jim came over. "I didn't see it," said Jim, "but if Luke says that's what happened, then that's what happened."

Ted and four security men arrived in a truck. It had a hoist on the front. One of the men agreed to go down into the hole on a rope.

Ted started the engine on the hoist and the man was slowly lowered down. He had taken another small rope to pull on for signalling.

Ted held the other end of the rope. Two tugs: That meant the man had reached the bottom. Three tugs meant to pull him up.

The man was pulled out of the hole. He was covered in mud from head to foot.

"Nothing down there except more mud," he said.

Luke couldn't believe it. The lights had been on. He had seen them go sliding down with his own eyes. "They must be there," he said. "You didn't look long enough. Let me go down!"

The foreman shook his head. "Then you'll refuse to come up again! Is that your plan to keep us from working here? I'm not falling for that one."

What happened next shouldn't have happened.

The only person that Luke had ever cared about, even if he hadn't been able to tell her, was gone. Lisa was gone. And here was a man with a sneering face calling Luke a liar.

Luke pushed the foreman down, hard. Two of Ted's men grabbed him and pulled him back. If the police hadn't arrived at that moment, Luke might have gotten into even more trouble.

Luke tried to calm down and explain what happened. But the police didn't believe him either. Even Big Jim was starting to doubt him.

"Are you sure, Luke?" asked Big Jim. "They said they weren't there. Even these guys wouldn't just leave them down there."

A police officer peered into the hole.

"You'd better take another look down there in the morning, just to be sure," he said.

The foreman was not in the mood to agree to anything.

"Fine," he said. "But it'll have to be early. Those scientists have decided that they're not interested in the hole after all. And tomorrow morning, I've got two truckloads of rock coming to fill it up. By tomorrow night, this will all just be a bad memory!"

Chapter 10

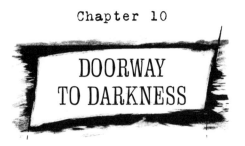

DOORWAY TO DARKNESS

Lisa was badly bruised when she got to the bottom of the hole. She had slid all the way down, and sharp stones had cut into her clothes.

She landed with a thump. For a minute she did not move or open her eyes. When she did, she saw a faint light. It came from a large square opening on the floor of the hole. She looked around for Harold, but there was no sign of him. He must have tumbled down farther, through the square opening.

Lisa shuddered. She didn't want to go through that opening. But Harold might need her help.

She crawled over to the square hole and looked down. She could see a rocky tunnel below. The walls glowed with a strange green light. In the dim light, she could see Harold lying on the ground.

"Here goes!" she said, and slipped through the tunnel feet first.

It was an odd feeling, jumping down into the tunnel. She felt dizzy and sick for a few seconds.

She tried very hard not to land on Harold. She hoped he wasn't hurt too badly. It would be very difficult getting such a big man out again.

As she reached Harold, he groaned and sat up.

"Are you all right, Mr. Dyson?" Lisa asked.

"I think so. I'm getting too old for this kind of thing. I'm banged up, but nothing is broken, thank goodness."

That was a relief. Lisa tried to help Harold stand up. It was a low tunnel, and he couldn't stand up straight.

"How are we going to get out of here?" said Lisa.

"Up the way we came," said Harold. "Through that square hole."

But when they looked up, the hole had disappeared. They could see nothing but a rocky ceiling. Harold banged on it, but everything seemed solid.

"We'd better see where this tunnel leads," he said.

Before they left the place, Harold stuck a piece of paper between two stones in the wall. "Just so we know where the doorway was," he said.

They walked quietly along the tunnel. After a short distance, the tunnel turned and stopped. A solid wall faced them.

"Let's try the other way," said Harold.

They turned and walked back. When they reached the piece of paper, they looked up hopefully. Had the doorway come back? No, the roof was as solid as ever.

Harold was finding it hard to walk. He had to stoop, which made his back ache. And even worse, they could smell the horrible stink of the scaly creatures.

Walking in the other direction, Harold and Lisa came to the tunnel opening quite suddenly. It was dark outside. Harold and Lisa pushed through a wall of bushes.

They found themselves on the side of a hill. There was no rain, and, strangely, the ground seemed quite dry. Stars twinkled through openings in the clouds. There was a strange scent in the air. It wasn't horrible like the creatures, but Lisa couldn't tell what it was.

By the faint starlight, they could see down into a wide valley. It was quiet. All they could hear was wind rustling through the bushes. It didn't look anything like Mott Hill or the campsite.

Suddenly Harold grabbed Lisa by the arm. He pointed up.

"Look," he said in a shaking voice.

Lisa looked up. The clouds were drifting away. Moonlight lit up the valley.

Lisa gasped.

There were two moons in the sky.

Chapter 11

UNDER THE TWO MOONS

The clouds were clearing, and Harold and Lisa could see more and more of the sky. The stars shined brightly. They seemed brighter than Lisa had ever seen them before.

"Where on Earth are we?" she said.

"That's just it," said Harold. "I don't think we are on Earth. Look at those moons, and the stars!"

"You mean, we're on Mars, or somewhere?" said Lisa. "That's just stupid!"

"Not Mars. The star patterns would look the same from Mars as they do from Earth. These stars look completely different," Harold said.

At one end of the valley, the sky seemed lighter. Morning was coming! Minute by minute, they could see more clearly.

"How can it be? How can we possibly travel millions and millions of miles just by jumping through a hole?" asked Lisa.

Harold shook his head. "I don't know. One thing I am sure of: Those creatures must live here. Maybe they passed through the doorway by mistake, just like we did."

Lisa nodded slowly. "Perhaps that's how people travel through space, through doorways that bend space around so you can travel anywhere in seconds."

"I saw a science fiction movie once where people could do that. Maybe the doorway on Earth has been forgotten and covered up for years and years," Harold said.

The sun came up. It seemed much bigger and brighter than the sun they were used to.

"I can't understand why the creatures hated the light," said Lisa. "You'd need sunglasses to live here."

"I guess they live underground, and only come out at night to hunt," said Harold. "With their big eyes, the moonlight and starlight would be very bright to them."

They could see right across the valley now. Tall, thin trees were scattered here and there. They had long, dark green leaves, and did not look like Earth trees at all.

Across the valley, they could see a giant pile of stones. It looked like the remains of a ruined castle. At the bottom of the valley there was a stream. A road ran along the side of it.

"Look at that," said Harold. "A road. That must mean people."

"How do you know they will be people?" said Lisa. "They might be anything. And they might be very unfriendly."

"Listen!" said Harold. "What's that sound?"

Figures appeared at the far end of the valley. It looked as if something was being slowly dragged along the ground. Lisa could hear shouts and a cracking sound.

"I think now would be a good time to hide," said Harold.

They hid behind the bushes and watched. The figures looked like the creatures that had attacked the camp. A group of them were dragging a huge wagon.

Another group sat in the wagon. They were dressed in blue uniforms. Now and then one of them yelled and cracked a whip at the creatures dragging the heavy wagon.

"Slaves!" whispered Harold. "So I guess these creatures are not friendly. We better keep quiet."

Lisa was crouched in an uncomfortable position. She moved her feet and stepped on a loose stone. Suddenly, she lost her balance and found herself sliding down the hillside!

A yell came from below. The creatures in blue took long weapons from the wagon and pointed them at Lisa.

Two of them started to run up the hill toward her.

"Hurry!" shouted Harold. "Back into the tunnel!"

As soon as they started to run for the tunnel, the creatures below started shouting and growling. Harold and Lisa reached the tunnel and scrambled inside.

"Come on," said Harold. "Maybe the doorway has opened again."

They raced down the tunnel. About halfway to the doorway, they stopped to listen. They heard shouting from behind them. The creatures were coming down the tunnel!

Then they heard another sound. A hissing and scraping sound came from up ahead of them. The doorway was open again, and the other creature had returned.

Chapter 12

THROUGH THE TUNNEL

"Quick," said Harold. "See if your flashlight is still working!"

Lisa switched her light on. Nothing happened. She gave it a bang and the light flashed on. Harold's light was working too.

They moved down the passage. The doorway was open again, and the creature crouched right underneath it. It didn't seem to know which way to go.

"Shine your light!" said Harold. "Drive it away, toward the dead end!"

The scaly creature squealed at the bright light and scurried along the tunnel. The smell was terrible in that small space.

"Now, quick," said Harold. "Up you go!"

Lisa climbed up through the opening. As she passed through, she felt dizzy and sick again. She turned to help Harold through. He found the climb difficult, but at last he did it. Puffing, they sat at the bottom of the hole in a huge puddle. Above them it was still night, but the rain had stopped.

Below, in the tunnel, they could hear shouts. Then, suddenly, the shouting stopped. The glowing light was gone.

The doorway was closed once more.

It was impossible to climb out of the deep, slippery hole. It was a long wait for daylight in the cold. They tried yelling for help, but there was no one to hear them.

At last, they heard noise from above: the roar of machinery, shouts and yells. Mud and small stones started to fall in on them. A bigger stone hit Lisa on the shoulder. Suddenly there were loud yells and a scuffling sound. Something was coming down the hole. Was there another creature on the loose?

It landed in a flurry of paws and a licking tongue.

"Raven," cried Lisa. "Oh, you wonderful, wonderful dog!"

It had been a close call.

The dump trucks had been about to tip their loads down the hole when Raven had rushed through the security men and jumped down it. Somehow he had known Lisa was down there.

The trucks were stopped and a man was sent down to rescue the dog. He was surprised to find two people there too.

Harold and Lisa were rushed to the hospital, but they only had cuts and bruises. Lisa had a nasty scratch on her shoulder from the creature.

Mike Short, from the radio station, wanted to hear their story, but Harold said that it would be better not to say too much.

Lisa agreed. Who would ever believe them anyway?

She didn't think that Luke would believe a word of it. After hitting the foreman, he had been taken to the police station to cool off in a cell.

When the news came that Lisa and Harold had been found in the hole, he was released without charge. He returned to the camp and found Lisa and Raven back in her old tent.

When Lisa had finished telling Luke her story, she looked at him. "I suppose you don't believe a word of it, do you?" she asked quietly.

Luke thought about it for a minute.

"That's always been my problem, hasn't it?" he said. "I've never believed in anything, not even myself."

He looked in her eyes. "Lisa, I was terrified when they couldn't find you down in that hole. Then I was locked up, so I couldn't hunt for you myself. I knew that the hole was going to be filled in. I thought I would never see you again."

From the direction of Mott Hill, the roar of machinery had started again. Suddenly the tent flap was pushed aside and Big Jim looked in.

"The work's started again," he said. "They'll be able to start building the road now that they've filled in the hole. Hurry up. You too, Raven. We've got some serious protesting to do!"

THE END

About the Author

David Orme, who also writes as John Banks, taught school for 18 years before becoming a full-time writer. He has written over 200 books about tornadoes, orangutans, soccer, space travel, and other topics. In his free time, David enjoys taking his granddaughter, Sarah, on adventures, climbing nearby mountains, and visiting city graveyards. He lives in Hampshire, England, with his wife, Helen, who is also a writer.

About the Illustrator

Sonny Liew was born in Malaysia, but he now lives in Singapore. He has worked on comics, computer games, and illustrations for many different comic and game publishers. He has been a featured illustrator in the critically acclaimed *Flight* series.

Glossary

cell (SEL)—a room in a prison or jail

drizzle (DRIZ-uhl)—a light, soft rain

foreman (FOR-mun)—the head of a team of workers

forensics (for-EN-ziks)—the science of examining dead bodies and discovering how they died

generator (JEN-uh-ray-tur)—an engine for creating electrical power

hoist (HOYST)—a machine used for lifting heavy objects or machinery

megaphone (MEG-uh-fohn)—a device shaped like a cone that is used to make a person's voice louder and stronger

muzzle (MUZZ-uhl)—straps that fit around an animal's head and mouth

protester (PRO-tess-tur)—someone who makes a strong statement or takes action against something

scramble (SKRAM-buhl)—to climb or move around clumsily

Discussion Questions

1. Why did Luke get so angry with the foreman and his workers after Lisa disappeared down the hole?

2. Harold Dyson had books that told about other strange things that had happened on Mott Hill, but no one believed him. Do you think the author of the story believes in weird things like this? Do you think the author had a reason for telling this story?

3. Luke had never had good friends before he met Lisa and Raven. Why do you think it took him so long to make friends?

Writing Prompts

1. The doorway at the bottom of the hole led Lisa and Harold to another world. Some people believe there are doorways between distant parts of outer space. These doorways are known as wormholes. What if you walked through a wormhole and ended up on another planet? What kind of things would you see? What kind of creatures live there? Describe your trip through one of these weird wormholes. Would you want to come back home?

2. The scaly creatures that came through the doorway killed some cows and attacked people. Do you think they did this on purpose? Were they frightened by being in a strange, new place? Imagine that you are one of these creatures, and describe your short visit to Earth.

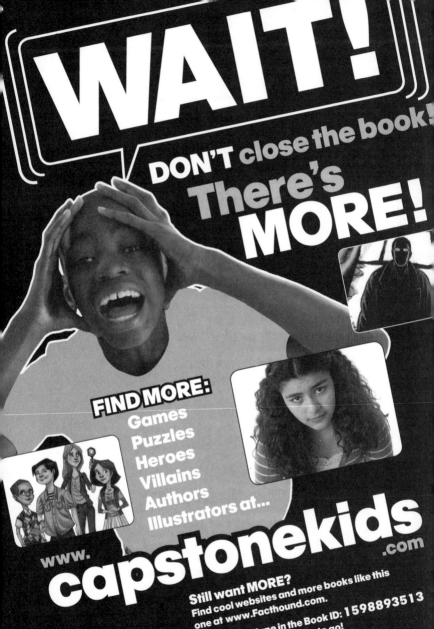